Night Flight

ANTOINE DE SAINT EXUPÉRY

Night Flight

Preface by André Gide
Translated from the French by Stuart Gilbert

A HARVEST/HBJ BOOK
HARCOURT BRACE JOVANOVICH, PUBLISHERS
NEW YORK AND LONDON

Published by arrangement with Editions Gallimard.

Printed in the United States of America

E F G H I J

Library of Congress Cataloging in Publication Data

Saint Exupéry, Antoine de, 1900–1944.
Night flight.

(A Harvest/HBJ book)
Reprint of the translation of Vol de nuit,
originally published by Reynal & Hitchcock, New York.
I.   Title.
PZ3.S137Ni10   [PQ2637.A274]   843'.9'12   73–16016
ISBN 0–15–665605–1

Night Flight

Preface

The *sine qua non* for the air-line companies was to compete in speed with all other systems of transport. In the course of this book Rivière, that leader to the manner born, sums up the issues. "It is a matter of life and death for us; for the lead we gain by day on ships and railways is lost each night." This night service—much criticized at the start but subsequently, once the experimental stage was over, accepted as a practical proposition—still involved at the time of this narrative considerable risks. For to the impalpable perils of all air routes and their manifold surprises accrued the night's dark treachery. I hasten to add that, great though these risks still are, they are growing daily less, for each successive trip facilitates and improves the prospects of the next one. Aviation, like the exploration of uncharted lands, has its early heroic age and "Night Flight," which describes the tragic adventure of one of these pioneers of the air, sounds, naturally enough, the authentic epic note.

The hero of "Night Flight," though human through and through, rises to superhuman heights of valor. The quality which I think delights one most of all in this stirring narrative is its nobility. Too well we know man's failings, his cowardice and lapses, and our writers of today are only too proficient in exposing these; but we stood in need of one to tell us how a man may be lifted far above himself by his sheer force of will.

More striking even than the aviator himself is, in my opinion, Rivière, his chief. The latter does not act, himself; he impels to action, breathes into his pilots his own virtue and exacts the utmost from them, constraining them to dare greatly. His iron will admits no flinching, and the least lapse is punished by him. At first sight his severity may seem inhuman and excessive. But its target is not the man himself, whom Rivière aspires to mold, but the man's blemishes. In his portrayal of this character we feel the author's profound admiration. I am especially grateful to him for bringing out a paradoxical truth which seems to me of great psychological import; that man's happiness lies not in freedom but in his acceptance of a duty. Each of the characters in this book is wholeheartedly, passionately devoted to that which duty bids him do, and it is in fulfilling this perilous task, and only thus, that he attains contentedness and peace. Reading between the lines we discover that Rivière is anything but insensitive (the narrative of his interview with the wife of the lost pilot is infinitely touching) and he needs quite as much courage to give his orders as the pilots need to carry them out.

"To make oneself beloved," he says, "one need only show pity. I show little pity, or I hide it. . . . My power sometimes amazes me." And, again: "Love the men under your orders, but do not let them know it."

A sense of duty commands Rivière in all things,

"the dark sense of duty, greater than that of love."
Man is not to seek an end within himself but to
submit and sacrifice his all to some strange thing
that commands him and lives through him. It
pleases me here to find that selfsame "dark sense"
which inspired my Prometheus to his paradox:
"Man I love not; I love that which devours him."
This is the mainspring of every act of heroism.
" 'We behave,' thought Rivière, 'as if there were
something of higher value than human life. . . . But
what thing?' " And again: "There is perhaps something else, something more lasting, to be saved;
and perhaps it was to save this part of man that
Rivière was working." A true saying.

In an age when the idea of heroism seems likely
to quit the army, since manly virtues may play
no part in those future wars whose horrors are
foreshadowed by our scientists, does not aviation
provide the most admirable and worthy field for
the display of prowess? What would otherwise be
rashness ceases to be such when it is part and
parcel of an allotted task. The pilot who is forever
risking his life may well smile at the current meaning we give to "courage." I trust that Saint Exupéry
will permit me to quote an old letter of his dating
from the time when he was flying on the Casa-
blanca–Dakar air route.

"I don't know when I shall be back, I have had
so much to do for several months, searches for
lost airmen, salvage of planes that have come
down in hostile territory, and some flights with
the Dakar mail.

"I have just pulled off a little exploit; spent two
days and nights with eleven Moors and a

mechanic, salving a plane. Alarums and excursions, varied and impressive. I heard bullets whizzing over my head for the first time. So now I know how I behave under such conditions; much more calmly than the Moors. But I also came to understand something which had always puzzled me—why Plato (Aristotle?) places courage in the last degree of virtues. It's a concoction of feelings that are not so very admirable. A touch of anger, a spice of vanity, a lot of obstinacy and a tawdry 'sporting' thrill. Above all, a stimulation of one's physical energies, which, however, is oddly out of place. One just folds one's arms, taking deep breaths, across one's opened shirt. Rather a pleasant feeling. When it happens at night another feeling creeps into it—of having done something immensely silly. I shall never again admire a merely brave man."

By way of epigraph I might append to this quotation an aphorism from Quinton's book (which, however, I cannot commend without reserve). "A man keeps, like his love, his courage dark." Or, better still: "Brave men hide their deeds as decent folk their alms. They disguise them or make excuses for them."

Saint Exupéry in all he tells us speaks as one who has "been through it." His personal contact with ever-recurrent danger seasons his book with an authentic and inimitable tang. We have had many stories of the War or of imaginary adventures which, if they showed the author as a man of nimble wit, brought smiles to the faces of such old soldiers or genuine adventurers as read them. I admire this work not only on its literary merits but for its value as a record of realities, and it is the unlikely combination of these two qualities which gives "Night Flight" its quite exceptional importance.

ANDRÉ GIDE

I

Already, beneath him, through the golden evening, the shadowed hills had dug their furrows and the plains grew luminous with long-enduring light. For in these lands the ground gives off this golden glow persistently, just as, even when winter goes, the whiteness of the snow persists.

Fabien, the pilot bringing the Patagonia air mail from the far south to Buenos Aires, could mark night coming on by certain signs that called to mind the waters of a harbor—a calm expanse beneath, faintly rippled by the lazy clouds—and he seemed to be entering a vast anchorage, an immensity of blessedness.

Or else he might have fancied he was taking a quiet walk in the calm of evening, almost like a shepherd. The Patagonian shepherds move, unhurried, from one flock to another; and he, too, moved from one town to another, the shepherd of those little towns. Every two hours he met another of them, drinking at its riverside or browsing on its plain.

Sometimes, after a hundred miles of steppes as desolate as the sea, he encountered a lonely farmhouse that seemed to be sailing backwards from him in a great prairie sea, with its freight of human lives; and he saluted with his wings this passing ship.

"San Julian in sight. In ten minutes we shall land."

The wireless operator gave their position to all the stations on the line. From Magellan Strait to Buenos Aires the airports were strung out across fifteen hundred miles and more, but this one led toward the frontiers of night, just as in Africa the last conquered hamlet opens onto the unknown.

The wireless operator handed the pilot a slip of paper: "There are so many storms about that the discharges are fouling my earphones. Shall we stop the night at San Julian?"

Fabien smiled; the sky was calm as an aquarium and all the stations ahead were signaling, *Clear sky: no wind.*

"No, we'll go on."

But the wireless operator was thinking: these storms had lodged themselves somewhere or other, as worms do in a fruit; a fine night, but they would ruin it, and he loathed entering this shadow that was ripe to rottenness.

As he slowed down his engine for the San Julian landing, Fabien knew that he was tired. All that endeared his life to man was looming up to meet him; men's houses, friendly little cafés, trees under which they walk. He was like some conqueror who, in the aftermath of victory, bends down upon his territories and now perceives the humble happiness of men. A need came over Fabien to lay his weapons down and feel the aching burden of his limbs—for even our misfortunes are a part of our belongings—and to stay, a simple dweller here, watching from his window a scene that would never change. This tiny village, he could gladly have made friends with it; the choice once made, a man accepts the issue of his venture and can love the life. Like love, it hems him in. Fabien would have wished to live a long while here—here to possess his morsel of eternity. These little towns, where he lived an hour, their gardens girdled by old walls over which he passed, seemed something apart and everlasting. Now the village was rising to meet the plane, opening out toward him. And there, he mused, were friendliness and gentle girls, white napery spread in quiet homes; all that is slowly shaped toward eternity. The village streamed past beneath his wings, yielding the secrets of closed gardens that their walls no longer guarded. He landed; and now he knew that he had seen nothing at all, only a few men slowly moving amongst their stones. The village kept, by its mere immobility, the secret of its passions and withheld its kindly charm; for, to master that, he would have needed to give up an active life.

The ten minutes' halt was ended and Fabien resumed his flight. He glanced back toward San Julian; all he now could see was a cluster of lights, then stars, then twinkling star dust that vanished, tempting him for the last time.

"I can't see the dials; I'll light up."

He touched the switches, but the red light falling from the cockpit lamps upon the dial hands was so diluted with the blue evening glow that they did not catch its color. When he passed his fingers close before a bulb, they were hardly tinged at all.

"Too soon."

But night was rising like a tawny smoke and already the valleys were brimming over with it. No longer were they distinguishable from the plains. The villages were lighting up, constellations that greeted each other across the dusk. And, at a touch of his finger, his flying-lights flashed back a greeting to them. The earth grew spangled with light signals as each house lit its star, searching the vastness of the night as a lighthouse sweeps the sea. Now every place that sheltered human life was sparkling. And it rejoiced him to enter into this one night with a measured slowness, as into an anchorage.

He bent down into the cockpit; the luminous dial hands were beginning to show up. The pilot read their figures one by one; all was going well. He felt at ease up here, snugly ensconced. He passed his fingers along a steel rib and felt the stream of life that flowed in it; the metal did not vibrate, yet it was alive. The engine's five-hundred horse-power bred in its texture a very gentle current, fraying its ice-cold rind into a velvety bloom. Once again the pilot in full flight experienced neither giddiness nor any thrill; only the mystery of metal turned to living flesh.

So he had found his world again. . . . A few digs of his elbow, and he was quite at home. He tapped the dashboard, touched the contacts one by one, shifting his limbs a little, and, settling himself more solidly, felt for the best position whence to gage the faintest lurch of his five tons of metal, jostled by the heaving darkness. Groping with his fingers, he plugged in his emergency lamp, let go of it, felt for it again, made sure it held; then lightly touched each switch, to be certain of finding it later, training his hands to function in a blind man's world. Now that his hands had learnt their role by heart, he ventured to turn on a lamp, making the cockpit bright with polished fittings and then, as on a submarine about to dive, watched his passage into night upon the dials only. Nothing shook or rattled, neither gyroscope nor altimeter flickered in the least, the engine was running smoothly; so now he relaxed his limbs a little, let his neck sink back into the leather padding and fell into the deeply meditative mood of flight, mellow with inexplicable hopes.

Now, a watchman from the heart of night, he learnt how night betrays man's presence, his voices, lights, and his unrest. That star down there in the shadows, alone; a lonely house. Yonder a fading star; that house is closing in upon its love. . . . Or on its lassitude. A house that has ceased to flash its signal to the world. Gathered round their lamp-lit table, those peasants do not know the measure of their hopes; they do not guess that their desire carries so far, out into the vastness of the night that hems them in. But Fabien has met it on his path, when, coming from a thousand miles away, he feels the heavy ground swell raise his panting plane and let it sink, when he has crossed a dozen storms like lands at war, between them neutral tracts of moonlight, to reach at last those lights, one following the other—and knows himself a conqueror. They think, these peasants, that their lamp shines only for that little table; but, from

fifty miles away, some one has felt the summons
of their light, as though it were a desperate signal
from some lonely island, flashed by shipwrecked
men toward the sea.

II

Thus the three planes of the air-mail service,
from Patagonia, Chile, and Paraguay, were con-
verging from south, west, and north on Buenos
Aires. Their arrival with the mails would give
the signal for the departure, about midnight, of
the Europe postal plane.

Three pilots, each behind a cowling heavy as a
river barge, intent upon his flight, were hastening
through the distant darkness, soon to come slowly
down, from a sky of storm or calm, like wild,
outlandish peasants descending from their high-
lands.

Rivière, who was responsible for the entire
service, was pacing to and fro on the Buenos
Aires landing ground. He was in silent mood, for,
till the three planes had come in, he could not
shake off a feeling of apprehension which had
been haunting him all day. Minute by minute, as
the telegrams were passed to him, Rivière felt
that he had scored another point against fate,
reduced the quantum of the unknown, and was
drawing his charges in, out of the clutches of
the night, toward their haven.

One of the hands came up to Rivière with a
radio message.

"Chile mail reports: Buenos Aires in sight."

"Good."

Presently, then, Rivière would hear its drone; already the night was yielding up one of them, as a sea, heavy with its secrets and the cadence of the tides, surrenders to the shore a treasure long the plaything of the waves. And soon the night would give him back the other two.

Then today's work would be over. Worn out, the crews would go to sleep, fresh crews replace them. Rivière alone would have no respite; then, in its turn, the Europe mail would weigh upon his mind. And so it would always be. Always. For the first time in his life this veteran fighter caught himself feeling tired. Never could an arrival of the planes mean for him the victory that ends a war and preludes a spell of smiling peace. For him it meant just one more step, with a thousand more to follow, along a straight, unending road. Rivière felt as though for an eternity he had been carrying a crushing load on his uplifted arms; an endless, hopeless effort.

"I'm aging." If he no longer found a solace in work and work alone, surely he was growing old. He caught himself puzzling over problems which hitherto he had ignored. There surged within his mind, like a lost ocean, murmuring regrets, all the gentler joys of life that he had thrust aside. "Can it be coming on me—so soon?" He realized that he had always been postponing for his declining years, "when I have time for it," everything that makes life kind to men. As if it were ever possible to "have time for it" one day and realize at life's end that dream of peace and happiness! No, peace there could be none; nor any victory, perhaps. Never could all the air mails land in one swoop once for all.

Rivière paused before Leroux; the old foreman was hard at work. Leroux, too, had forty years of work behind him. All his energies were for his work. When at ten o'clock or midnight Leroux went home it certainly was not to find a change of scene, escape into another world. When Rivière smiled toward him, he raised his heavy head and pointed at a burnt-out axle. "Jammed it was, but I've fixed it up." Rivière bent down to look; duty had regained its hold upon him. "You should tell the shop to set them a bit looser." He passed his finger over the trace of seizing, then glanced again at Leroux. As his eyes lingered on the stern old wrinkled face, an odd question hovered on his lips and made him smile.

"Ever had much to do with love, Leroux, in your time?"

"Love, sir? Well, you see—"

"Hadn't the time for it, I suppose—like me."

"Not a great deal, sir."

Rivière strained his ears to hear if there were any bitterness in the reply; no, not a trace of it. This man, looking back on life, felt the quiet satisfaction of a carpenter who has made a good job of planing down a board: "There you are! *That's* done."

"There you are," thought Rivière. "My life's done."

Then, brushing aside the swarm of somber thoughts his weariness had brought, he walked toward the hangar; for the Chile plane was droning down toward it.

III

The sound of the distant engine swelled and thickened; a sound of ripening. Lights flashed out. The red lamps on the light-tower silhouetted a hangar, radio standards, a square landing ground. The setting of a gala night.

"There she comes!"

A sheaf of beams had caught the grounding plane, making it shine as if brand-new. No sooner had it come to rest before the hangar than mechanics and airdrome hands hurried up to unload the mail. Only Pellerin, the pilot, did not move.

"Well, aren't you going to get down?"

The pilot, intent on some mysterious task, did not deign to reply. Listening, perhaps, to sounds that he alone could hear, long echoes of the flight. Nodding reflectively, he bent down and tinkered with some unseen object. At last he turned toward the officials and his comrades, gravely taking stock of them as though of his possessions. He seemed to pass them in review, to weigh them, take their measure, saying to himself that he had earned his right to them, as to this hangar with its gala lights and solid concrete and, in the offing, the city, full of movement, warmth, and women. In the hollow of his large hands he seemed to hold this folk; they were his subjects, to touch or hear or curse, as the fancy took him. His impulse now was to curse them for a lazy crowd, so sure of life they seemed, gaping at the moon; but he decided to be genial instead.

". . . Drinks are on you!"

Then he climbed down.

He wanted to tell them about the trip.

"If only you knew . . . !"

Evidently, to his thinking, that summed it up,
for now he walked off to change his flying gear.

As the car was taking him to Buenos Aires in
the company of a morose inspector and Rivière
in silent mood, Pellerin suddenly felt sad; of
course, he thought, it's a fine thing for a fellow
to have gone through it and, when he's got his
footing again, let off a healthy volley of curses.
Nothing finer in the world! But afterwards . . .
when you look back on it all; you wonder, you
aren't half so sure!

A struggle with a cyclone, that at least is a
straight fight, it's *real*. But not that curious look
things wear, the face they have when they think
they are alone. His thoughts took form. "Like a
revolution it is; men's faces turning only the least
shade paler, yet utterly unlike themselves."

He bent his mind toward the memory.

He had been crossing peacefully the Cordillera
of the Andes. A snow-bound stillness brooded on
the ranges; the winter snow had brought its
peace to all this vastness, as in dead castles the
passing centuries spread peace. Two hundred
miles without a man, a breath of life, a movement; only sheer peaks that, flying at twenty
thousand feet, you almost graze, straight-falling
cloaks of stone, an ominous tranquility.

It had happened somewhere near the Tupun-
gato Peak. . . .

He reflected. . . . Yes, it was there he saw a
miracle take place.

For at first he had noticed nothing much, felt
no more than a vague uneasiness—as when a
man believes himself alone, but is not; some one
is watching him. Too late, and how he could not
comprehend, he realized that he was hemmed in
by anger. Where was it coming from, this anger?
What told him it was oozing from the stones,
sweating from the snow? For nothing seemed on
its way to him, no storm was lowering. And still
—another world, like it and yet unlike, was issu-
ing from the world around him. Now all those
quiet-looking peaks, snowcaps, and ridges, growing faintly grayer, seemed to spring to life, a
people of the snows. And an inexplicable anguish
gripped his heart.

Instinctively he tightened his grasp on the controls. Something he did not understand was on
its way and he tautened his muscles, like a beast
about to spring. Yet, as far as eye could see, all
was at peace. Peaceful, yes, but tense with some
dark potency.

Suddenly all grew sharp; peaks and ridges
seemed keen-edged prows cutting athwart a heavy
head wind. Veering around him, they deployed
like dreadnoughts taking their positions in a battle
line. Dust began to mingle with the air, rising and
hovering, a veil above the snow. Looking back to
see if retreat might still be feasible, he shuddered;
all the Cordillera behind him was in seething fer-
ment.

"I'm lost!"

On a peak ahead of him the snow swirled up into the air—a snow volcano. Upon his right flared up another peak and, one by one, all the summits grew lambent with gray fire, as if some unseen messenger had touched them into flame. Then the first squall broke and all the mountains round the pilot quivered.

Violent action leaves little trace behind it and he had no recollection of the gusts that buffeted him then from side to side. Only one clear memory remained; the battle in a welter of gray flames.

He pondered.

"A cyclone, that's nothing. A man just saves his skin! It's what comes before it—the thing one meets upon the way!"

But already, even as he thought he had recalled it, that one face in a thousand, he had forgotten what it was like.

IV

Rivière glanced at the pilot. In twenty minutes Pellerin would step from the car, mingle with the crowd, and know the burden of his lassitude. Perhaps he would murmur: "Tired out as usual. It's a dog's life!" To his wife he would, perhaps, let fall a word or two: "A fellow's better off here than flying above the Andes!" And yet that world to which men hold so strongly had almost slipped from him; he had come to know its wretchedness. He had returned from a few hours' life on the other side of the picture, ignoring if it would be possible for him ever to retrieve this city with its lights, ever to know again his little human frailties, irksome yet cherished childhood friends.

"In every crowd," Rivière mused, "are certain persons who seem just like the rest, yet they bear amazing messages. Unwittingly, no doubt, unless —" Rivière was chary of a certain type of admirers, blind to the higher side of this adventure, whose vain applause perverted its meaning, debased its human dignity. But Pellerin's inalienable greatness lay in this—his simple yet sure awareness of what the world, seen from a special angle, signified, his massive scorn of vulgar flattery. So Rivière congratulated him: "Well, how did you bring it off?" And loved him for his knack of only "talking shop," referring to his flight as a blacksmith to his anvil.

Pellerin began by telling how his retreat had been cut off. It was almost as if he were apologizing about it. "There was nothing else for it!" Then he had lost sight of everything, blinded by the snow. He owed his escape to the violent air currents which had driven him up to twenty-five thousand feet. "I guess they held me all the way just above the level of the peaks." He mentioned his trouble with gyroscope and how he had had to shift the air-inlet, as the snow was clogging it; "forming a frost glaze, you see." After that another set of air currents had driven Pellerin down and, when he was only at ten thousand feet or so, he was puzzled why he had not run into anything. As a matter of fact he was already above the plains. "I spotted it all of a sudden when I came out into a clear patch." And he explained how it had felt at that moment; just as if he had escaped from a cave.

"Storm at Mendoza, too?"

"No. The sky was clear when I made my landing, not a breath of wind. But the storm was at my heels all right!"

It was such a damned queer business, he said; that was why he mentioned it. The summits were lost in snow at a great height while the lower slopes seemed to be streaming out across the plain, like a flood of black lava which swallowed up the villages one by one. "Never saw anything like it before. . . ." Then he relapsed into silence, gripped by some secret memory.

Rivière turned to the inspector.

"That's a Pacific cyclone; it's too late to take any action now. Anyhow these cyclones never cross the Andes."

No one could have foreseen that this particular cyclone would continue its advance toward the east.

The inspector, who had no ideas on the subject, assented.

The inspector seemed about to speak. Then he hesitated, turned toward Pellerin, and his Adam's apple stirred. But he held his peace and, after a moment's thought, resumed his air of melancholy dignity, looking straight before him.

That melancholy of his, he carried it about with him everywhere, like a handbag. No sooner had he landed in Argentina than Rivière had appointed him to certain vague functions, and now his large hands and inspectorial dignity got always in his way. He had no right to admire imagination or ready wit; it was his business to commend punctuality and punctuality alone. He had no right to take a glass of wine in company, to call a comrade by his Christian name or risk a joke; unless, of course, by some rare chance, he came across another inspector on the same run.

"It's hard luck," he thought, "always having to be a judge."

As a matter of fact he never judged; he merely wagged his head. To mask his utter ignorance he would slowly, thoughtfully, wag his head at everything that came his way, a movement that struck fear into uneasy consciences and ensured the proper upkeep of the plant.

He was not beloved—but then inspectors are not made for love and such delights, only for drawing up reports. He had desisted from proposing changes of system or technical improvements since Rivière had written: *Inspector Robineau is requested to supply reports, not poems. He will be putting his talents to better use by speeding up the personnel.* From that day forth Inspector Robineau had battened on human frailties, as on his daily bread; on the mechanic who had a glass too much, the airport overseer who stayed up of nights, the pilot who bumped a landing.

Rivière said of him: "He is far from intelligent, but very useful to us, such as he is." One of the rules which Rivière rigorously imposed—upon himself—was a knowledge of his men. For Robineau the only knowledge that counted was knowledge of the *orders*.

"Robineau," Rivière had said one day, "you must cut the punctuality bonus whenever a plane starts late."

"Even when it's nobody's fault? In case of fog, for instance?"

"Even in case of fog."

Robineau felt a thrill of pride in knowing that his chief was strong enough not to shrink from being unjust. Surely Robineau himself would win reflected majesty from such overweening power!

"You postponed the start till six fifteen," he would say to the airport superintendents. "We cannot allow your bonus."

"But, Monsieur Robineau, at five thirty one couldn't see ten yards ahead!"

"Those are the *orders*."

"But, Monsieur Robineau, we couldn't sweep the fog away with a broom!"

He alone amongst all these nonentities knew the secret; if you only punish men enough, the weather will improve!

"He never thinks at all," said Rivière of him, "and that prevents him from thinking wrong."

The pilot who damaged a plane lost his no-accident bonus.

"But supposing his engine gives out when he is over a wood?" Robineau inquired of his chief.

"Even when it occurs above a wood."

Robineau took to heart the *ipse dixit*.

"I regret," he would inform the pilots with cheerful zest, "I regret it very much indeed, but you should have had your breakdown somewhere else."

"But, Monsieur Robineau, one doesn't choose the place to have it."

"Those are the orders."

The orders, thought Rivière, are like the rites of a religion; they may look absurd but they shape men in their mold. It was no concern to Rivière whether he seemed just or unjust. Perhaps the words were meaningless to him. The little towns-folk of the little towns promenade each evening round a bandstand and Rivière thought: It's non-sense to talk of being just or unjust toward them; they don't exist.

For him, a man was a mere lump of wax to be kneaded into shape. It was his task to furnish this dead matter with a soul, to inject will power into it. Not that he wished to make slaves of his men; his aim was to raise them above themselves. In punishing them for each delay he acted, no doubt, unjustly, but he bent the will of every crew to punctual departure; or, rather, he bred in them the will to keep to time. Denying his men the right to welcome foggy weather as the pretext for a leisure hour, he kept them so breathlessly eager for the fog to lift that even the humblest mechanic felt a twinge of shame for the delay. Thus they were quick to profit by the least rift in the armor of the skies.

"An opening on the north; let's be off!"

Thanks to Rivière the service of the mails was paramount over twenty thousand miles of land and sea.

"The men are happy," he would say, "because they like their work, and they like it because I am hard."

And hard he may have been—still he gave
his men keen pleasure for all that. "They need," he
would say to himself, "to be urged on toward a
hardy life, with its sufferings and its joys; only
that matters."

As the car approached the city, Rivière in-
structed the driver to take him to the Head Office.
Presently Robineau found himself alone with
Pellerin and a question shaped itself upon his
lips.

V

Robineau was feeling tired tonight. Looking at
Pellerin—Pellerin the Conqueror—he had just discovered that his own life was a gray one. Worst
of all, he was coming to realize that, for all his
rank of inspector and authority, he, Robineau,
cut a poor figure beside this travel-stained and
weary pilot, crouching in a corner of the car, his
eyes closed and hands all grimed with oil. For the
first time, Robineau was learning to admire. A
need to speak of this came over him and, above
all, to make a friend.

He was tired of his journey and the day's rebuffs
and felt perhaps a little ridiculous. That very evening, when verifying the gasoline reserve, he had
botched his figures and the agent, whom he had
wanted to catch out, had taken compassion and
totted them up for him. What was worse, he had
commented on the fitting of a Model B.6 oil pump,
mistaking it for the B.4 type, and the mechanics

with ironic smiles had let him maunder on for twenty minutes about this "inexcusable stupidity" —his own stupidity.

He dreaded his room at the hotel. From Toulouse to Buenos Aires, straight to his room he always went once the day's work was over. Safely ensconced and darkly conscious of the secrets he carried in his breast, he would draw from his bag a sheet of paper and slowly inscribe *Report* on it, write a line or two at random, then tear it up. He would have liked to save the company from some tremendous peril; but it was not in any danger. All he had saved so far was a slightly rusted propeller-boss. He had slowly passed his finger over the rust with a mournful air, eyed by an airport overseer, whose only comment was: "Better call up the last halt; this plane's only just in." Robineau was losing confidence in himself.

At a venture he essayed a friendly move. "Would you care to dine with me?" he asked Pellerin. "I'd enjoy a quiet chat; my job's pretty exhausting at times."

Then, reluctant to quit his pedestal too soon, he added: "The responsibility, you know."

His subordinates did not much relish the idea of intimacy with Robineau; it had its dangers. "If he's not dug up something for his report, with an appetite like his, I guess he'll just eat me up!"

But Robineau's mind this evening was full of his personal afflictions. He suffered from an annoying eczema, his only real secret; he would have liked to talk about his trouble, to be pitied and, now that pride had played him false, find solace in humility. Then again there was his mistress over

there in France, who had to hear the nightly tale
of his inspections whenever he returned. He
hoped to impress her thus and earn her love—
his usual luck!—he only seemed to aggravate her.
He wanted to talk about her, too.

"So you'll come to dinner?"

Good-naturedly Pellerin assented.

VI

The clerks were drowsing in the Buenos Aires
office when Rivière entered. He had kept his overcoat and hat on, like the incessant traveler he
always seemed to be. His spare person took up
so little room, his clothes and graying hair so
aptly fitted into any scene, that when he went by
hardly any one noticed it. Yet, at his entry, a wave
of energy traversed the office. The staff bustled,
the head clerk hurriedly compiled the papers re-
maining on his desk, typewriters began to click.
The telephonist was busily slipping his plugs
into the standard and noting the telegrams in a
bulky register. Rivière sat down and read them.

All that he read, the Chile episode excepted, told
of one of those favored days when things go right
of themselves and each successive message from
the airports is another bulletin of victory. The
Patagonia mail, too, was making headway; all the
planes were ahead of time, for fair winds were
bearing them northward on a favoring tide.

"Give me the weather reports."

Each airport vaunted its fine weather, clear sky,

and clement breeze. The mantle of a golden evening had fallen on South America. And Rivière welcomed this friendliness of things. True, one of the planes was battling somewhere with the perils of the night, but the odds were in its favor.

Rivière pushed the book aside.

"That will do."

Then, a night warden whose charge was half the world, he went out to inspect the men on night duty, and came back.

Later, standing at an open window, he took the measure of the darkness. It contained Buenos Aires yonder, but also, like the hull of some huge ship, America. He did not wonder at this feeling of immensity; the sky of Santiago de Chile might be a foreign sky, but once the air mail was in flight toward Santiago you lived, from end to journey's end, under the same dark vault of heaven. Even now the Patagonian fishermen were gazing at the navigation lights of the plane whose messages were being awaited here. The vague unrest of an airplane in flight brooded not only on Rivière's heart but, with the droning of the engine, upon the capitals and little towns.

Glad of this night that promised so well, he recalled those other nights of chaos, when a plane had seemed hemmed in with dangers, its rescue well-nigh a forlorn hope, and how to the Buenos Aires Radio Post its desperate calls came faltering through, fused with the atmospherics of the storm. Under the leaden weight of sky the golden music of the waves was tarnished. Lament in the minor of a plane sped arrowwise against the blinding barriers of darkness, no sadder sound than this!

Rivière remembered that the place of an inspector, when the staff is on night duty, is in the office.

"Send for Monsieur Robineau."

Robineau had all but made a friend of his guest, the pilot. Under his eyes he had unpacked his suitcase and revealed those trivial objects which link inspectors with the rest of men; some shirts in execrable taste, a dressing set, the photograph of a lean woman, which the inspector pinned to the wall. Humbly thus he imparted to Pellerin his needs, affections, and regrets. Laying before the pilot's eyes his sorry treasures, he laid bare all his wretchedness. A moral eczema. His prison.

But a speck of light remained for Robineau, as for every man, and it was in a mood of quiet ecstasy that he drew, from the bottom of his valise, a little bag carefully wrapped up in paper. He fumbled with it some moments without speaking. Then he unclasped his hands.

"I brought this from the Sahara."

The inspector blushed to think that he had thus betrayed himself. For all his chagrins, domestic misadventures, for all the gray reality of life he had a solace, these little blackish pebbles—talismans to open doors of mystery.

His blush grew a little deeper. "You find exactly the same kind in Brazil."

Then Pellerin had slapped the shoulder of an

inspector poring upon Atlantis and, as in duty
bound, had asked a question.

"Keen on geology, eh?"

"Keen? I'm mad about it!"

All his life long only the stones had not been
hard on him.

Hearing that he was wanted, Robineau felt sad
but forthwith resumed his air of dignity.

"I must leave you. Monsieur Rivière needs my
assistance for certain important problems."

When Robineau entered the office, Rivière had
forgotten all about him. He was musing before a
wall map on which the company's airlines were
traced in red. The inspector awaited his chief's
orders. Long minutes passed before Rivière addressed him, without turning his head.

"What is your idea of this map, Robineau?"

He had a way of springing conundrums of this
sort when he came out of a brown study.

"The map, Monsieur Rivière? Well—"

As a matter of fact he had no ideas on the subject; nevertheless, frowning at the map, he roved
all Europe and America with an inspectorial eye.
Meanwhile Rivière, in silence, pursued his train of
thought. "On the face of it, a pretty scheme enough
—but it's ruthless. When one thinks of all the
lives, young fellows' lives, it has cost us! It's a fine,
solid thing and we must bow to its authority, of
course; but what a host of problems it presents!"
With Rivière, however, nothing mattered save the
end in view.

Robineau, standing beside him with his eyes

fixed on the map, was gradually pulling himself together. Pity from Rivière was not to be expected; that he knew. Once he had chanced it, explaining how that grotesque infirmity of his had spoilt his life. All he had got from Rivière was a jeer. "Stops you sleeping, eh? So much the better for your work!"

Rivière spoke only half in jest. One of his sayings was: "If a composer suffers from loss of sleep and his sleeplessness induces him to turn out masterpieces, what a profitable loss it is!" One day, too, he had said of Leroux: "Just look at him! I call it a fine thing, ugliness like that—so perfect that it would warn off any sweetheart!" And perhaps, indeed, Leroux owed what was finest in him to his misfortune, which obliged him to live only for his work.

"Pellerin's a great friend of yours, isn't he, Robineau?"

"Well—"

"I'm not reproaching you."

Rivière made a half-turn and with bowed head, taking short steps, paced to and fro with Robineau. A bitter smile, incomprehensible to Robineau, came to his lips.

"Only . . . only you are his chief, you see."

"Yes," said Robineau.

Rivière was thinking how tonight, as every night, a battle was in progress in the southern sky. A moment's weakening of the will might spell defeat; there was, perhaps, much fighting to be done before the dawn.

"You should keep your place, Robineau." Rivière weighed his words. "You may have to order this pilot tomorrow night to start on a dangerous flight. He will have to obey you."

"Yes."

"The lives of men worth more than you are in your hands." He seemed to hesitate. "It's a serious matter."

For a while Rivière paced the room in silence, taking his little steps.

"If they obey you because they like you, Robineau, you're fooling them. You have no right to ask any sacrifice of them."

"No, of course not."

"And if they think that your friendship will get them off disagreeable duties, you're fooling them again. They have to obey in any case. Sit down."

With a touch of his hand Rivière gently propelled Inspector Robineau toward the desk.

"I am going to teach you a lesson, Robineau. If you feel run down it's not these men's business to give you energy. You are their chief. Your weakness is absurd. Now write!"

"I—"

"Write. *Inspector Robineau imposes the penalty stated hereunder on Pellerin, Pilot, on the following grounds. . . .* You will discover something to fill in the blanks."

"Sir!"

"Act as though you understood, Robineau. Love the men under your orders—but do not let them know it."

So, once more, Robineau would supervise the cleaning of each propeller-boss, with zest.

———

An emergency landing ground sent in a radio message. *Plane in sight. Plane signals: Engine Trouble; about to land.*

That meant half an hour lost. Rivière felt that mood of irritation the traveler knows when his express is held up by a signal and the minutes no longer yield their toll of passing hedgerows. The large clock hand was turning now an empty hemicycle, within whose compass so many things might have fitted in. To while away the interval Rivière went out and now the night seemed hollow as a stage without an actor. Wasted—a night like this! He nursed a grudge against the cloudless sky with its wealth of stars, the moon's celestial beacon, the squandered gold of such a night. . . .

But, once the plane had taken off, the night once more grew full of beauty and enthralment; for now the womb of night was carrying life, and over it Rivière kept his watch.

"What weather have you?"

He had the query transmitted to the crew. Ten seconds later the reply came in: "Very fine."

There followed a string of names, towns over which the plane had passed and, for Rivière's ears, these were so many names of cities falling one by one before a conqueror.

VII

An hour later the wireless operator on the Patagonia mail felt himself gently lifted as though some one were tugging at his shoulder. He looked around; heavy clouds were putting out the stars.

He leaned toward the earth, trying to see the village lights, shining like glowworms in the grass, but in those fields of darkness no light sparkled.

He felt depressed; a hard night lay before him, marches and countermarches, advances won and lost. He did not understand the pilot's tactics; a little further on and they would hit against that blackness, like a wall.

On the rim of the horizon in front he now could see a ghostly flicker, like the glow above a smithy. He tapped Fabien's shoulder, but the pilot did not stir.

Now the first eddies of the distant storm assailed them. The mass of metal heaved gently up, pressing itself against the operator's limbs; and then it seemed to melt away, leaving him for some seconds floating in the darkness, levitated. He clung to the steel bulwarks with both hands. The red lamp in the cockpit was all that remained to him of the world of men and he shuddered to know himself descending helpless into the dark heart of night, with only a little thing, a miner's safety lamp, to see him through. He dared not disturb the pilot to ask his plans; he tightened his grip on the steel ribs and, bending forward, fixed his eyes upon the pilot's shadowed back.

In that obscurity the pilot's head and shoulders were all that showed themselves. His torso was a block of darkness, inclined a little to the left; his face was set toward the storm, bathed intermittently, no doubt, by flickering gleams. He could not see that face; all the feelings thronging there to meet the onset of the storm were hidden from his eyes; lips set with anger and resolve, a white face holding elemental colloquy with the leaping flashes ahead.

Yet he divined the concentrated force that brooded in that mass of shadow, and he loved it. True, it was carrying him toward the tempest, yet it shielded him. True, those hands, gripping the controls, pressed heavy on the storm, as on some huge beast's neck, but the strong shoulders never budged, attesting vast reserves of force. And after all, he said to himself, the pilot's responsible. So, carried like a pillion-rider on this breakneck gallop into the flames, he could relish to its full the solid permanence, the weight and substance implicit in that dark form before him.

On the left, faint as a far revolving light, a new storm center kindled.

The wireless operator made as if to touch Fabien's shoulder and warn him, but then he saw him slowly turn his head, fix his eyes a while on this new enemy and then as slowly return to his previous position, his neck pressed back against the leather pad, shoulders unmoving as before.

VIII

Rivière went out for a short walk, hoping to shake off his malaise, which had returned. He who had only lived for action, dramatic action, now felt a curious shifting of the crisis of the drama, toward his own personality. It came to him that the little people of these little towns, strolling around their bandstands, might seem to lead a placid life and yet it had its tragedies; illness, love, bereavements, and that perhaps— His own trouble was teaching him many things, "opening windows," as he put it to himself.

Toward eleven he was breathing more easily and turned back toward the offices, slowly shouldering his way through the stagnant crowds around the cinemas. He glanced up at the stars which glinted on the narrow street, well-nigh submerged by glaring sky signs, and said to himself: "Tonight, with my two air mails on their way, I am responsible for all the sky. That star up there is a sign that is looking for me amongst this crowd—and finds me. That's why I'm feeling out of things, a man apart."

A phrase of music came back to him, some notes from a sonata which he had heard the day before in the company of friends. They had not understood. "That stuff bores us and bores you too, only you won't admit it!"

"Perhaps," he had replied.

Then, as tonight, he had felt lonely, but soon had learnt the bounty of such loneliness. The music had breathed to him its message, to him alone amongst these ordinary folk, whispered its gentle secret. And now the star. Across the shoulders of these people a voice was speaking to him in a tongue that he alone could understand.

On the pavement they were hustling him about. "No," he said to himself, "I won't get annoyed. I am like the father of a sick child walking in the crowd, taking short steps, who carries in his breast the hushed silence of his house."

He looked upon the people, seeking to discover

which of them, moving with little steps, bore in
his heart discovery or love—and he remembered
the lighthouse-keeper's isolation.

Back in the office, the silence pleased him. As
he slowly walked from one room to another, his
footsteps echoed emptiness. The typewriters slept
beneath their covers. The big cupboard doors
were closed upon the serried files. Ten years of
work and effort. He felt as if he were visiting the
cellars of a bank where wealth lies heavy on the
earth. But these registers contained a finer stuff
than gold—a stock of living energy, living but,
like the hoarded gold of banks, asleep.

Somewhere he would find the solitary clerk on
night duty. Somewhere here a man was working
that life and energy should persevere and thus the
work goes on from post to post that, from Toulouse to Buenos Aires, the chain of flights should
stay unbroken.

"That fellow," thought Rivière, "doesn't know
his greatness."

Somewhere, too, the planes were fighting forward; the night flights went on and on like a
persistent malady, and on them watch must be
kept. Help must be given to these men who with
hands and knees and breast to breast were wres-
tling with the darkness, who knew and only knew
an unseen world of shifting things, whence they
must struggle out, as from an ocean. And the
things they said about it afterwards were—ter-
rible! "I turned the light on to my hands so as to
see them." Velvet of hands bathed in a dim red

dark-room glow; last fragment, that must be saved, of a lost world.

Rivière opened the door of the Traffic Office. A solitary lamp shone in one corner, making a little pool of light. The clicking of a single typewriter gave meaning to the silence, but did not fill it. Sometimes the telephone buzzed faintly and the clerk on duty rose obedient to its sad, reiterated call. As he took down the receiver that invisible distress was soothed and a gentle, very gentle murmur of voices filled the coign of shadow.

Impassive the man returned to his desk, for drowsiness and solitude had sealed his features on a secret unconfessed. And yet—what menace it may hold, a call from the outer darkness when two postal planes are on their way! Rivière thought of telegrams that invaded the peace of families sitting round their lamp at night and that grief which, for seconds that seem unending, keeps its secret on the father's face. Waves, so weak at first, so distant from the call they carry, and so calm; and yet each quiet purring of the bell held, for Rivière, a faint echo of that cry. Each time the man came back from the shadow toward his lamp, like a diver returning to the surface, the solitude made his movements heavy with their secret, slow as a swimmer's in the undertow.

"Wait! I'll answer."

Rivière unhooked the receiver and a world of murmurs hummed in his ears.

"Rivière speaking."

Confused sounds, then a voice: "I'll put you on the radio station."

A rattle of plugs into the standard, then another voice: "Radio Station speaking. I'll pass you the messages."

Rivière noted them, nodding. "Good. . . . Good . . ."

Nothing important, the usual routine news. Rio de Janeiro asking for information, Montevideo reporting on the weather, Mendoza on the plant. Familiar sounds.

"And the planes?" he asked.

"The weather's stormy. We don't hear them tonight."

"Right!"

The night is fine here and starry, Rivière thought, yet those fellows can detect in it the breath of the distant storm.

"That's all for the present," he said.

As Rivière rose the clerk accosted him: "Papers to sign, sir."

Rivière discovered that he greatly liked this subordinate of his who was bearing, too, the brunt of night. "A comrade in arms," he thought. "But he will never guess, I fancy, how tonight's vigil brings us near each other."

IX

As he was returning to his private office, a sheaf of papers in his hand, Rivière felt the stab of pain in his right side which had been worrying him for some weeks past.

"That's bad. . . ."

He leaned against the wall a moment.

"It's absurd!"

Then he made his way to his chair.

Once again he felt like some old lion fallen in a trap and a great sadness came upon him.

"To think I've come to this after all those years of work! I'm fifty; all that time I've filled my life with work, trained myself, fought my way, altered the course of events and here's this damned thing getting a hold of me, obsessing me till it seems the only thing that matters in the world. It's absurd!"

He wiped away a drop or two of sweat, waited till the pain had ebbed and settled down to work, examining the memoranda on his table.

"In taking down Motor 301 at Buenos Aires we discovered that . . . The employee responsible will be severely punished."

He signed his name.

"The Florianopolis staff, having failed to comply with orders . . . "

He signed.

"As a disciplinary measure Airport Supervisor Richard, is transferred on the following grounds. . . . "

He signed.

Then, as the pain in his side, slumbering but persistent, new as a new meaning in life, drove his thoughts inward toward himself, an almost bitter mood came over him.

"Am I just or unjust? I've no idea. All I know is that when I hit hard there are fewer accidents. It isn't the individual that's responsible but a

sort of hidden force and I can't get at it without
—getting at every one! If I were merely just, every
night flight would mean a risk of death."

A sort of disgust came over him, that he had
given himself so hard a road to follow. Pity is a
fine thing, he thought. Lost in his musings, he
turned the pages over.

"Roblet, as from this day, is struck off the
strength. . . ."

He remembered the old fellow and their talk
the evening before.

"There's no way out of it, an example must be
made."

"But, sir. . . . It was the only time, just once in
a way, sir . . . and I've been hard at it all my life!"

"An example must be made."

"But . . . but, sir. Please see here, sir."

A tattered pocketbook, a newspaper picture
showing young Roblet standing beside an airplane. Rivière saw how the old hands were trembling upon this little scrap of fame.

"It was in nineteen ten, sir. That was the first
plane in Argentina and I assembled it. I've been
in aviation since nineteen ten, think of it, sir!
Twenty years! So how can you say . . . ? And
the young 'uns, sir, won't they just laugh about
it in the shop! Won't they just chuckle!"

"I can't help that."

"And my kids, sir. I've a family."

"I told you you could have a job as a fitter."

"But there's my good name, sir, my name . . .
after twenty years' experience. An old employee
like me!"

"As a fitter."

"No, sir, I can't see my way to that. I somehow can't, sir!"

The old hands trembled and Rivière averted his eyes from their plump, creased flesh which had a beauty of its own.

"No, sir, no. . . . And there's something more I'd like to say."

"That will do."

Not he, thought Rivière, it wasn't he whom I dismissed so brutally, but the mischief for which, perhaps, he was not responsible, though it came to pass through him. For, he mused, we can command events and they obey us; and thus we are creators. These humble men, too, are things and we create them. Or cast them aside when mischief comes about through them.

"There's something more I'd like to say." What did the poor old fellow want to say? That I was robbing him of all that made life dear? That he loved the clang of tools upon the steel of airplanes, that all the ardent poetry of life would now be lost to him . . . and then, a man must live?

"I am very tired," Rivière murmured and his fever rose, insidiously caressing him. "I liked that old chap's face." He tapped the sheet of paper with his finger. It came back to him, the look of the old man's hands and he now seemed to see them shape a faltering gesture of thankfulness. "That's all right," was all he had to say. "That's right. Stay!" And then—He pictured the torrent of joy that would flow through those old hands. Nothing in all the world, it seemed to him, could be more beautiful than that joy revealed not on a face, but in those toil-worn hands. Shall I tear up this paper? He imagined the old man's home-coming to his family, his modest pride.

"So they're keeping you on?"

"What do you think? It was I who assembled the first plane in Argentina!"

The old fellow would get back his prestige, the youngsters cease to laugh.

As he was asking himself if he would tear it up, the telephone rang.

There was a long pause, full of the resonance and depth that wind and distance give to voices.

"Landing ground speaking. Who is there?"

"Rivière."

"No. 650 is on the tarmac, sir."

"Good."

"We've managed to fix it up, but the electric circuit needed overhauling at the last minute, the connections had been bungled."

"Yes. Who did the wiring?"

"We will inquire and, if you agree, we'll make an example. It's a serious matter when the lights give out on board."

"You're right."

If, Rivière was thinking, one doesn't uproot the mischief whenever and wherever it crops up, the lights may fail and it would be criminal to let it pass when, by some chance, it happens to un-mask its instrument; Roblet shall go.

The clerk, who had noticed nothing, was busy with his typewriter.

"What's that?"

"The fortnightly accounts."

"Why not ready?"

"I . . . I . . ."

"We'll see about that."

Curious, mused Rivière, how things take the upper hand, how a vast dark force, the force that thrusts up virgin forests, shows itself whenever a great work is in the making! And he thought of temples dragged asunder by frail liana tendrils.

A great work. . . .

And, heartening himself, he let his thought flow on. These men of mine, I love them; it's not they whom I'm against, but what comes about through them. . . . His heart was throbbing rapidly and it hurt him. . . . No, I cannot say if I am doing right or what precise value should be set on a human life, or suffering, or justice. How should I know the value of a man's joys? Or of a trembling hand? Of kindness, or pity?

Life is so full of contradictions; a man muddles through it as best he can. But to endure, to create, to barter this vile body. . . .

As if to conclude his musings he pressed the bell-push.

"Ring up the pilot of the Europe mail and tell him to come and see me before he leaves."

For he was thinking: I must make sure he doesn't turn back needlessly. If I don't stir my men up the night is sure to make them nervous.

X

Roused by the call, the pilot's wife looked musingly at her husband. I'll let him sleep a bit longer, she thought.

She admired that spanned bared chest of his

and the thought came to her of a well-built ship. In the quiet bed, as in a harbor, he was sleeping and, lest anything should spoil his rest, she smoothed out a fold of the sheet, a little wave of shadow, with her hand, bringing calm upon the bed, as a divine hand calms the sea.

Rising, she opened the window and felt the wind on her face. Their room overlooked Buenos Aires. A dance was going on in a house near by and the music came to her upon the wind, for this was the hour of leisure and amusement. In a hundred thousand barracks this city billeted its men and all was peaceful and secure; but, the woman thought, soon there'll be a cry "To arms!" and only one man—mine—will answer it. True, he rested still, yet his was the ominous rest of reserves soon to be summoned to the front. This town at rest did not protect him; its light would seem as nothing when, like a young god, he rose above its golden dust. She looked at the strong arms which, in an hour, would decide the fortune of the Europe mail, bearing a high responsibility, like a city's fate. The thought troubled her. That this man alone, amongst those millions, was destined for the sacrifice made her sad. It estranged him from her love. She had cherished him, watched over him, caressed him, not for herself but for this night which was to take him. For struggles, fears, and victories which she would never know. Wild things they were, those hands of his, and only tamed to tenderness; their real task was dark to her. She knew this man's smile, his gentle ways of love, but not his godlike fury in the storm. She might snare him in a fragile net of music, love, and flowers, but, at each departure, he would break forth without, it seemed to her, the least regret.

He opened his eyes. "What time is it?"

"Midnight."

"How's the weather?"

"I don't know."

He rose and, stretching himself, walked to the window. "Won't be too cold. What's the wind?"

"How should I know?"

He leaned out. "Southerly. That's tophole. It'll hold as far as Brazil anyhow."

He looked at the moon and reckoned up his riches and then his gaze fell upon the town below. Not warm or kind or bright it seemed to him; already in his mind's eye its worthless, shining sands were running out.

"What are you thinking about?"

He was thinking of the fog he might encounter toward Porto Allegre.

"I've made my plans. I know exactly where to turn."

He still was bending down, inhaling deeply like a man about to plunge, naked, into the sea.

"You don't even seem to mind it! How long will you be away?" she asked.

A week or ten days, he couldn't say. "Mind it?" Why should he? All those cities, plains, and mountains. . . . In freedom he was going out to conquer them. In under an hour, he thought, he would have annexed Buenos Aires and tossed it aside!

He smiled at his thoughts. This town . . . it will soon be left behind. It's fine starting out at night.

One opens out the gas, facing south, and ten seconds later swings the landscape roundabout, heading up north. The town looks like the bottom of the sea.

She thought of all a man must lay aside to conquer. "So you don't like your home?"

"I do like my home."

But his wife knew that he was already on his way and even now his sturdy shoulders were pressing up against the sky.

She pointed to the sky. "A fine night. See, your road is paved with stars!"

He laughed. "Yes."

She rested her hand on his shoulder and its moist warmth disquieted her; did some danger threaten this young flesh of his?

"I know how strong you are, but—do take care!"

"Of course I'll take care."

Then he began dressing. For the occasion he chose the coarsest, roughest fabrics, the heaviest of leather—a peasant's kit. The heavier he grew, the more she admired him. Herself she buckled his belt, helped to pull his boots on.

"These boots pinch me!"

"Here are the others."

"Bring a cord for my emergency lamp."

She looked at him, set to rights the last flaw in his armor; all fell into place.

"You look splendid."

Then she noticed that he was carefully brushing his hair.

"For the benefit of the stars?" she questioned.

"I don't want to feel old."

"I'm jealous."

He laughed again and kissed her, pressing her to his heavy garments. Then he lifted her from the ground between his outstretched arms, like a little girl, and, laughing still, deposited her on the bed.

"Go to sleep!"

He shut the door behind him and, passing amongst the indistinguishable folk of night, took the first step toward his conquests.

She remained, sadly looking at these flowers and books, little friendly things which meant for him no more than the bottom of the sea.

XI

Rivière greeted him.

"That's a nice trick you played on me, your last trip! You turned back though the weather reports were good. You could have pushed through all right. Got the wind up?"

Surprised, the pilot found no answer. He slowly rubbed his hands one on the other. Then, raising his head, he looked Rivière in the eyes.

"Yes," he answered.

Deep in himself Rivière felt sorry for this brave fellow who had been afraid. The pilot tried to explain.

"I couldn't see a thing. No doubt, further on . . . perhaps . . . the radio said. . . . But my lamp was getting weak and I couldn't see my hands. I tried turning on my flying-light so as to spot a wing anyhow, but I saw nothing. It was like being at the bottom of a huge pit, and no getting out of it. Then my engine started a rattle."

"No."

"No?"

"No, we had a look at it. In perfect order. But a man always thinks the engine's rattling when he gets the wind up."

"And who wouldn't? The mountains were above me. When I tried to climb I got caught in heavy squalls. When one can't see a damned thing, squalls, you know. . . . Instead of climbing I lost three hundred feet or more. I couldn't even see the gyroscope or the manometers. It struck me that the engine was running badly and heating up, and the oil pressure was going down. And it was dark as a plague of Egypt. Damned glad I was to see the lights of a town again."

"You've too much imagination. That's what it is."

The pilot left him.

Rivière sank back into the armchair and ran his fingers through his grizzled hair.

The pluckiest of my men, he thought. *It was a fine thing he did that night, but I've stopped him from being afraid.*

He felt a mood of weakness coming over him again.

To make oneself beloved one need only show pity. I show little pity, or I hide it. Sure enough it would be fine to create friendships and human kindness around me. A doctor can enjoy that in the course of his profession. But I'm the servant of events and, to make others serve them too, I've got to temper my men like steel. That dark necessity is with me every night when I read over the flight reports. If I am slack and let events take charge, trusting to routine, always mysteriously something seems to happen. It is as if my will alone forbade the plane in flight from breaking or the storm to hold the mail up. My power sometimes amazes me.

His thoughts flowed on.

Simple enough, perhaps. Like a gardener's endless labor on his lawn; the mere pressure of his hand drives back into the soil the virgin forest which the earth will engender time and time again.

His thoughts turned to the pilot.

I am saving him from fear. I was not attacking *him* but, across him, that stubborn inertia which paralyzes men who face the unknown. If I listen and sympathize, if I take his adventure seriously, he will fancy he is returning from a land of mystery, and mystery alone is at the root of fear. We must do away with mystery. Men who have gone down into the pit of darkness must come up and say—there's nothing in it! This man must enter the inmost heart of night, that clotted darkness, without even his little miner's davy, whose light, falling only on a hand or wing, suffices to push the unknown a shoulder's breath away.

Yet a silent communion, deep within them, united Rivière and his pilots in the battle. All were like shipmates, sharing a common will to victory.

Rivière remembered other battles he had joined to conquer night. In official circles darkness was dreaded as a desert unexplored. The idea of

launching a craft at a hundred and fifty miles
an hour against the storm and mists and all the
solid obstacles night veils in darkness might suit
the military arm; you leave on a fine night, drop
bombs and return to your starting point. But
regular night services were doomed to fail. "It's
a matter of life and death," said Rivière, "for the
lead we gain by day on ships and railways is lost
each night."

Disgusted, he had heard them prate of balance
sheets, insurance, and, above all, public opinion.
"Public opinion!" he exclaimed. "The public does
as it's told!" But it was all waste of time, he was
saying to himself. There's something far above
all that. A living thing forces its way through,
makes its own laws to live and nothing can resist
it. Rivière had no notion when or how commercial
aviation would tackle the problem of night flying
but its inevitable solution must be prepared for.

Those green tablecloths over which he had
leaned, his chin propped on his arm, well he
remembered them! And his feeling of power as
he heard the others' quibbles! Futile these had
seemed, doomed from the outset by the force of
life. He felt the weight of energy that gathered in
him. And I shall win, thought Rivière, for the
weight of argument is on my side. That is the
natural trend of things. They urged him to pro-
pose a utopian scheme, devoid of every risk.
"Experience will guide us to the rules," he said.
"You cannot make rules precede practical experience."

After a hard year's struggles, Rivière got his
way. "His faith saw him through," said some, but

others: "No, his tenacity. Why, the fellow's as obstinate as a bear!" But Rivière put his success down to the fact that he had lent his weight to the better cause.

Safety first was the obsession of those early days. Planes were to leave only an hour before dawn, to land only an hour after sunset. When Rivière felt surer of his ground, then and only then did he venture to send his planes into the depth of night. And now, with few to back him, disowned by nearly all, he plowed a lonely furrow.

Rivière rang up to learn the latest messages from the planes in flight.

XII

Now the Patagonia mail was entering the storm and Fabien abandoned all idea of circumventing it; it was too widespread for that, he reckoned, for the vista of lightning flashes led far inland, exposing battlement on battlement of clouds. He decided to try passing below it, ready to beat a retreat if things took a bad turn.

He read his altitude, five thousand five hundred feet, and pressed the controls with his palms to bring it down. The engine started thudding violently, setting all the plane aquiver. Fabien corrected the gliding angle approximately, verifying on the map the height of the hills, some sixteen hundred feet. To keep a safety margin he determined to fly at a trifle above two thousand, staking his altitude as a gambler risks his fortune.

An eddy dragged him down, making the plane tremble still more harshly and he felt the threat of unseen avalanches that toppled all about him. He dreamt an instant of retreat and its guerdon of a hundred thousand stars, but did not shift his course by one degree.

Fabien weighed his chances; probably this was just a local storm, as Trelew, the next halt, was signaling a sky only three-quarters overcast. A bare twenty minutes more of solid murk and he would be through with it. Nevertheless the pilot felt uneasy. Leaning to his left, to windward, he sought to catch those vague gleams which, even in darkest nights, flit here and there. But even those vagrant gleams were gone; at most there lingered patches in the mass of shadow where the night seemed less opaque, or was it only that his eyes were growing strained?

The wireless operator handed him a slip of paper.

"Where are we?"

Fabien would have given much to know. "Can't say exactly," he answered. "We are flying by compass across a storm."

He leaned down again. The flame from the exhaust was getting on his nerves. There it was, clinging to the motor like a spray of fireflowers, so pale it seemed that moonlight would have quelled it, but, in this nothingness, engulfing all the visible world. He watched it streaming stiffly out into the wind, like a torch flame.

Every thirty seconds Fabien bent down into the cockpit to check the gyroscope and compass. He dared not light the dim red lamps which would have dazzled his eyes for some moments, but the luminous dial hands were ceaselessly emitting their pale and starry radiance. And in all those needles and printed figures the pilot found an illusive reassurance, as in the cabin of a ship swept by the waves. For, like a very sea of strange fatality, the night was rolling up against him with all its rocks and reefs and wreckage.

"Where are we?" the operator asked again.

Fabien drew himself up and, leaning to the left, resumed his tremendous vigil. He had no notion left how many hours more and what efforts would be needed to deliver him from fettering darkness. Would he ever come clear, he wondered, for he was staking his life on this little slip of dirty, crumpled paper, which he unfolded and re-read a thousand times to nurse his hopes: *Trelew. Sky three-quarters overcast. Westerly breeze.* If there still remained a clear patch over Trelew, he would presently glimpse its lights across a cloud rift. Unless. . . .

That promise of a faint gleam far ahead beckoned him on; but, to make sure, he scribbled a message to the radio operator. "Don't know if I can get through. Ask if the weather's holding out behind."

The answer appalled him.

"Commodoro reports: Impossible return here. Storm."

He was beginning to measure this unforeseen offensive, launched from the Cordillera toward the sea. Before he could make them the storm would have burst upon the cities.

"Get the San Antonio weather report."

"San Antonio reports: West wind rising. Storm in the west. Sky three-quarters overcast. San Antonio picking up badly on account of interferences. I'm having trouble too. I shall have to pull up the aerial on account of the lightning. Will you turn back? What are your plans?"

"Stow your damned questions! Get Bahia Blanca!"

"Bahia Blanca reports: Violent westerly gale over Bahia Blanca expected in less than twenty minutes."

"Ask Trelew."

"Trelew reports: Westerly gale; a hundred feet per second; rain squalls."

"Inform Buenos Aires: We are cut off on all sides; storm developing over a depth of eight hundred miles; no visibility. What shall we do?"

A shoreless night, the pilot thought, leading to no anchorage (for every port was unattainable, it seemed), nor toward dawn. In an hour and twenty minutes the fuel would run out. Sooner or later he must blindly founder in the sea of darkness. Ah, if only he could have won through to daylight!

Fabien pictured the dawn as a beach of golden sand where a man might get a foothold after this hard night. Beneath him the plains, like friendly shores, would spread their safety. The quiet land would bear its sleeping farms and flocks and hills. And all the flotsam swirling in the shadows would lose its menace. If it were possible, how gladly he would swim toward the strand of daylight! But, well he knew, he was surrounded; for better or

for worse the end would come within this murk
of darkness. . . . Sometimes, indeed, when daybreak came, it seemed like convalescence after
illness.

What use to turn his eyes toward the east, home
of the sun? Between them lay a gulf of night so
deep that he could never clamber up again.

XIII

"The Asuncion mail is making good headway;
it should be in at about two. The Patagonia mail,
however, seems to be in difficulties and we expect
it to be much overdue."

"Very good, Monsieur Rivière."

"Quite possibly we won't make the Europe mail
wait for it; as soon as Asuncion's in, come for in-
structions, please. Hold yourself in readiness."

Rivière read again the weather reports from
the northern sectors. "Clear sky; full moon; no
wind." The mountains of Brazil were standing
stark and clear against the moonlit sky, the
tangled tresses of their jet-black forests falling
sheer into a silver tracery of sea. Upon those
forests the moonbeams played and played in vain,
tingeing their blackness with no light. Black, too,
as drifting wreckage, the islands flecked the sea.
But all the outward air route was flooded by that
exhaustless fountain of moonlight.

If Rivière now gave orders for the start, the
crew of the Europe mail would enter a stable
world, softly illuminated all night long. A land
which held no threat for the just balance of light

and shade, unruffled by the least caress of those cool winds which, when they freshen, can ruin a whole sky in an hour or two.

Facing this wide radiance, like a prospector eyeing a forbidden gold field, Rivière hesitated. What was happening in the south put Rivière, sole protagonist of night flights, in the wrong. His opponents would make such moral capital out of a disaster in Patagonia that all Rivière's faith would henceforth be unavailing. Not that his faith wavered; if, through a fissure in his work, a tragedy had entered in, well, the tragedy might prove the fissure—but it proved nothing else. Perhaps, he thought, it would be well to have look-out posts in the west. That must be seen to. "After all," he said to himself, "my previous arguments hold good as ever and the possibilities of accident are reduced by one, the one tonight has illustrated." The strong are strengthened by reverses; the trouble is that the true meaning of events scores next to nothing in the match we play with men. Appearances decide our gains or losses and the points are trumpery. And a mere semblance of defeat may hopelessly checkmate us.

He summoned an employee. "Still no radio from Bahia Blanca?"

"No."

"Ring up the station on the phone."

Five minutes later he made further inquiries. "Why don't you pass on the messages?"

"We can't hear the mail."

"He's not sending anything?"

"Can't say. Too many storms. Even if he was sending we shouldn't pick it up."

"Can you get Trelew?"

"We can't hear Trelew."

"Telephone."

"We've tried. The line's broken."

"How's the weather your end?"

"Threatening. Very sultry. Lightning in the west and south."

"Wind?"

"Moderate so far. But in ten minutes the storm will break; the lightning's coming up fast."

Silence.

"Hullo, Bahia Blanca! You hear me? Good. Call me again in ten minutes."

Rivière looked through the telegrams from the southern stations. All alike reported: No message from the plane. Some had ceased by now to answer Buenos Aires and the patch of silent areas was spreading on the map as the cyclone swept upon the little towns and one by one, behind closed doors, each house along the lightless streets grew isolated from the outer world, lonely as a ship on a dark sea. And only dawn would rescue them.

Rivière, poring on the map, still hoped against hope to discover a haven of clear sky, for he had telegraphed to the police at more than thirty up-country police stations and their replies were coming in. And the radio posts over twelve hundred miles of country had orders to advise Buenos Aires within thirty seconds if any message from the plane was picked up, so that Fabien might learn at once whither to fly for refuge.

The employees had been warned to attend at I A.M. and were now at their posts. Somehow,

mysteriously, a rumor was gaining ground that
perhaps the night flights would be suspended in
future and the Europe mail would leave by day.
They spoke in whispers of Fabien, the cyclone
and, above all, of Rivière whom they pictured
near at hand and point by point capitulating to
this rebuff the elements had dealt.

Their chatter ceased abruptly; Rivière was
standing at his door, his overcoat tight-buttoned
across his chest, his hat well down upon his
eyes, like the incessant traveler he always seemed.
Calmly he approached the head clerk.

"It's one ten. Are the papers for the Europe mail
in order?"

"I—I thought—"

"Your business is to carry out orders, not to
think."

Slowly turning away, he moved toward an open
window, his hands clasped behind his back. A
clerk came up to him.

"We have very few replies, sir. We hear that a
great many telegraph lines in the interior have
been destroyed."

"Right!"

Unmoving, Rivière stared out into the night.

Thus each new message boded new peril for the
mail. Each town, when a reply could be sent
through before the lines were broken, announced
the cyclone on its way, like an invading horde.
"It's coming up from the Cordillera, sweeping
everything before it, toward the sea."

To Rivière the stars seemed over-bright, the air
too moist. Strange night indeed! It was rotting

away in patches, like the substance of a shining
fruit. The stars, in all their host, still looked down
on Buenos Aires—an oasis, and not to last. A
haven out of Fabien's range, in any case. A night
of menace, touched and tainted by an evil wind.
A difficult night to conquer.

Somewhere in its depths an airplane was in
peril; here, on the margin, they were fighting to
rescue it, in vain.

XIV

Fabien's wife telephoned.

Each night she calculated the progress of the
homing Patagonia mail. "He's leaving Trelew
now," she murmured. Then went to sleep again.
Presently: "He's getting near San Antonio, he has
its lights in view." Then she got out of bed, drew
back the curtains and summed up the sky. "All
those clouds will worry him." Sometimes the moon
was wandering like a shepherd and the young
wife was heartened by the faithful moon and
stars, the thousand presences that watched her
husband. Toward one o'clock she felt him near
her. "Not far to go, Buenos Aires is in sight."
Then she got up again, prepared a meal for him,
a nice steaming cup of coffee. "It's so cold up
there!" She always welcomed him as if he had
just descended from a snow peak. "You *must* be
cold!" "Not a bit." "Well, warm yourself anyhow!"
She had everything ready at a quarter past one.
Then she telephoned. Tonight she asked the usual
question.

"Has Fabien landed?"

The clerk at the other end grew flustered. "Who's speaking?"

"Simone Fabien."

"Ah! A moment, please. . . . "

Afraid to answer, he passed the receiver to the head clerk.

"Who's that?"

"Simone Fabien."

"Yes. What can I do for you?"

"Has my husband arrived?"

After a silence which must have baffled her, there came a monosyllable. "No."

"Is he delayed?"

"Yes."

Another silence. "Yes, he is delayed."

"Ah!"

The cry of a wounded creature. A little delay, that's nothing much, but when it lasts, when it lasts. . . .

"Yes. And when—when is he expected in?"

"When is he expected? We . . . we don't know exactly . . . "

A solid wall in front of her, a wall of silence, which only gave her back the echo of her questions.

"Do please tell me, where is he now?"

"Where is he? Wait. . . . "

This suspense was like a torture. Something was happening there, behind that wall.

At last, a voice! "He left Commodoro at seven thirty this evening."

"Yes? And then?"

"Then—delayed, seriously delayed by stormy weather."

"Ah! A storm!"

The injustice of it, the sly cruelty of that moon up there, that lazing moon of Buenos Aires! Suddenly she remembered that it took barely two hours to fly from Commodoro to Trelew.

"He's been six hours on the way to Trelew! But surely you've had messages from him. What does he say?"

"What does he say? Well, you see, with weather like that . . . it's only natural . . . we can't hear him."

"Weather like—?"

"You may rest assured, madame, the moment we get news of him, we will ring you up."

"Ah! You've no news."

"Good night, madame."

"No! No! I want to talk to the director."

"I'm sorry, he's very busy just now; he has a meeting on—"

"I can't help that. That doesn't matter. I insist on speaking to him."

The head clerk mopped his forehead. "A moment, please."

He opened Rivière's door.

"Madame Fabien wants to speak to you, sir."

"Here," thought Rivière, "is what I was dreading." The emotional elements of the drama were coming into action. His first impulse was to thrust them aside; mothers and women are not allowed in an operating theater. And all emotion is bidden to hold its peace on a ship in peril; it

does not help to save the crew. Nevertheless he
yielded.

"Switch on to my phone."

No sooner did he hear that far off, quavering
voice, than he knew his inability to answer it. It
would be futile for both alike, worse than futile,
to meet each other.

"Do not be alarmed, madame, I beg you. In
our calling it so often happens that a long while
passes without news."

He had reached a point where not the problem
of a small personal grief but the very will to act
was in itself an issue. Not so much Fabien's wife
as another theory of life confronted Rivière now.
Hearing that timid voice, he could but pity its
infinite distress—and know it for an enemy! For
action and individual happiness have no truck
with each other; they are eternally at war. This
woman, too, was championing a self-coherent
world with its own rights and duties, that world
where a lamp shines at nightfall on the table,
flesh calls to mated flesh, a homely world of
love and hopes and memories. She stood up for
her happiness and she was right. And Rivière,
too, was right, yet he found no words to set
against this woman's truth. He was discovering
the truth within him, his own inhuman and unutterable truth, by an humble light, the lamplight
of a little home!

"Madame . . . !"

She did not hear him. Her hands were bruised
with beating on the wall and she lay fallen, or
so it seemed to him, almost at his feet.

———

One day an engineer had remarked to Rivière, as they were bending above a wounded man, beside a bridge that was being erected: "Is the bridge worth a man's crushed face?" Not one of the peasants using the road would ever have wished to mutilate this face so hideously just to save the extra walk to the next bridge. "The welfare of the community," the engineer had continued, "is just the sum of individual welfares and has no right to look beyond them." "And yet," Rivière observed on a subsequent occasion, "even though human life may be the most precious thing on earth, we always behave as if there were something of higher value than human life. . . . But what thing?"

Thinking of the lost airmen, Rivière felt his heart sink. All man's activity, even the building of a bridge, involves a toll of suffering and he could no longer evade the issue—"Under what authority?"

These men, he mused, who perhaps are lost, might have led happy lives. He seemed to see as in a golden sanctuary the evening lamplight shine on faces bending side by side. "Under what authority have I taken them from all this?" he wondered. What was his right to rob them of their personal happiness? Did not the highest of all laws ordain that these human joys should be safeguarded? But he destroyed them. And yet one day, inevitably, those golden sanctuaries vanish like mirage. Old age and death, more pitiless than even he, destroy them. There is, perhaps, some other thing, something more lasting, to be saved; and, perhaps, it was to save this part of man that Rivière was working. Otherwise there could be no defense for action.

To love, only to love, leads nowhere. Rivière knew a dark sense of duty, greater than that of love. And deep within it there might lie another emotion and a tender one, but worlds away from ordinary feelings. He recalled a phrase that he once had read: "The one thing is to make them everlasting. . . . That which you seek within yourself will die." He remembered a temple of the sun god, built by the ancient Incas of Peru. Tall menhirs on a mountain. But for these what would be left of all that mighty civilization which with its massive stones weighs heavy, like a dark regret, on modern man? Under the mandate of what strange love, what ruthlessness, did that primeval leader of men compel his hordes to drag this temple up the mountainside, bidding them raise up their eternity? And now another picture rose in Rivière's mind; the people of the little towns, strolling by nights around their bandstands. That form of happiness, those shackles . . . he thought. The leader of those ancient races may have had scant compassion for man's sufferings, but he had a boundless pity for his death. Not for his personal death, but pity for his race, doomed to be blotted out beneath a sea of sand. And so he bade his folk set up these stones at least, something the desert never would engulf.

XV

That scrap of folded paper might perhaps save him yet; gritting his teeth, Fabien unfolded it.

"Impossible communicate Buenos Aires. Can't even touch the key, the shocks are numbing my hands."

In his vexation Fabien wanted to reply, but the moment his hands left the controls to write, a vast ground swell seemed to surge up across his body; the eddies lifted him in his five tons of metal and rocked him to and fro. He abandoned the attempt.

Again he clenched his hands upon the tempest and brought it down. Fabien was breathing heavily. If that fellow pulled up the aerial for fear of the storm, Fabien would smash his face in when they landed. At all costs they must get in touch with Buenos Aires—as though across the thousand miles and more a safety line might be flung to rescue them from this abyss! If he could not have one vagrant ray of light, not even the flicker of an inn-lamp—of little help indeed, yet shining like a beacon, earnest of the earth—at least let him be given a voice, a single word from that lost world of his. The pilot raised his fist and shook it in the red glow, hoping to make the man behind him understand the tragic truth, but the other was bending down to watch a world in ruins, with its buried cities and dead lights, and did not see him.

Let them shout any order whatever to him and Fabien would obey. *If they tell me to go round and* round, he thought, I'll turn in circles and if they say I must head due south. . . . For somewhere, even now, there still were lands of calm, at peace beneath the wide moon shadows. His comrades down there, omniscient folk like clever scientists, knew all about them, poring upon the maps beneath their hanging lamps, pretty as flower-bells. But he, what could he know save squalls and night, this night that buffeted him with its swirling spate of darkness? Surely they could not leave two men to their fate in these whirlwinds and flaming clouds! No, that was unthinkable! They might order Fabien to set his course at two hundred and forty degrees, and he would do it. . . . But he was alone.

It was as if dead matter were infected by his exasperation; at every plunge the engine set up such furious vibrations that all the fuselage seemed convulsed with rage. Fabien strained all his efforts to control it; crouching in the cockpit, he kept his eyes fixed on the artificial horizon only, for the masses of sky and land outside were not to be distinguished, lost both alike in a welter as of worlds in the making. But the hands of the flying instruments oscillated more and more abruptly, grew almost impossible to follow. Already the pilot, misled by their vagaries, was losing altitude, fighting against odds, while deadly quicksands sucked him down into the darkness. He read his height, sixteen hundred—just the level of the hills. He guessed their towering billows hard upon him, for now it seemed that all these earthen monsters, the least of which could crush him into nothingness, were breaking loose from their foundations and careering about in a drunken frenzy. A dark tellurian carnival was thronging closer and closer round him.

He made up his mind. He would land no matter where, even if it meant cracking up! To avoid the hills anyhow, he launched his only landing flare. It sputtered and spun, illumining a vast plain, then died away; beneath him lay the sea!

His thoughts came quickly. Lost—forty degrees' drift—yes, I've drifted, sure enough—it's a cyclone—where's land? He turned due west. Without another flare, he thought, I'm a goner. Well, it was bound to happen one day. And that fellow behind there! Sure thing he's pulled up the aerial. . . . But now the pilot's anger had ebbed away. He had only to unclasp his hands and their lives would slither through his fingers like a trivial mote of dust. He held the beating heart of each —his own, his comrade's—in his hands. And suddenly his hands appalled him.

In these squalls that battered on the plane, to counteract the jerks of the wheel, which else would have snapped the control cables, he clung to it with might and main, never relaxing his hold for an instant. But now he could no longer feel his hands, numbed by the strain. He tried to shift his fingers and get some signal they were there, but he could not tell if they obeyed his will. His arms seemed to end in two queer foreign bodies, insentient like flabby rubber pads. "Better try hard to think I'm gripping," he said to himself. But whether his thought carried as far as his hands he could not guess. The tugs upon the wheel were only felt by him as sudden twinges in his shoulders. "I'll let go for sure. My fingers will open." His rashness scared him—that he had dared to even think such words!—for now he fancied that his hands, yielding to the dark suggestion of his thought, were opening slowly, slowly opening in the shadow, to betray him.

He might keep up the struggle, chance his luck; no destiny attacks us from outside. But, within him, man bears his fate and there comes a moment when he knows himself vulnerable; and then, as in a vertigo, blunder upon blunder lures him.

And, at this very moment, there gleamed above his head, across a storm rift, like a fatal lure within a deep abyss, a star or two.

Only too well he knew them for a trap. A man sees a few stars at the issue of a pit and climbs toward them, and then—never can he get down again but stays up there eternally, chewing the stars. . . .

But such was his lust for light that he began to climb.

XVI

He climbed and it grew easier to correct the plunges for the stars gave him his bearings. Their pale magnet drew him up; after that long and bitter quest for light, for nothing in the world would he forego the frailest gleam. If the glimmer of a little inn were all his riches, he would turn around this token of his heart's desire until his death! So now he soared toward the fields of light.

Little by little he spiraled up, out of the dark pit which closed again beneath him. As he rose the clouds began to shed their slime of shadow, flowing past him in cleaner, whiter billows. Fabien rose clear.

And now a wonder seized him; dazzled by that brightness, he had to keep his eyes closed for some seconds. He had never dreamt the night clouds could dazzle thus. But the full moon and all the constellations were changing them to waves of light.

In a flash, the very instant he had risen clear, the pilot found a peace that passed his understanding. Not a ripple tilted the plane but, like a ship that has crossed the bar, it moved across a tranquil anchorage. In an unknown and secret corner of the sky it floated, as in a harbor of the Happy Isles. Below him still the storm was fashioning another world, thridded with squalls and cloudbursts and lightnings, but turning to the stars a face of crystal snow.

Now all grew luminous, his hands, his clothes, the wings, and Fabien thought that he was in a limbo of strange magic; for the light did not come down from the stars but welled up from below, from all that snowy whiteness.

The clouds beneath threw up the flakes the moon was pouring on them; on every hand they loomed like towers of snow. A milky stream of light flowed everywhere, laving the plane and crew. When Fabien turned he saw the wireless operator smile.

"That's better!" he cried.

But his words were drowned by the rumor of the flight; they conversed in smiles. I'm daft, thought Fabien, to be smiling, we're lost.

And yet—at last a myriad dark arms had let him go; those bonds of his were loosed, as of a prisoner whom they let walk a while in liberty amongst the flowers.

"Too beautiful," he thought. Amid the far-flung treasure of the stars he roved, in a world where no life was, no faintest breath of life, save his and his companion's. Like plunderers of fabled cities they seemed, immured in treasure vaults whence there is no escape. Amongst these frozen jewels they were wandering, rich beyond all dreams, but doomed.

XVII

One of the wireless operators at the Commodoro Rivadavia station in Patagonia made a startled gesture and all the others keeping helpless vigil there crowded round to read the message.

A harsh light fell upon the blank sheet of paper over which they bent. The operator's hand seemed loath to do its task and his pencil shook. The words to write were prisoned in his hand, but already his fingers twitched.

"Storms?"

He nodded assent; he could hardly hear for interferences. Then he scrawled some illegible signs, then words; then, at last, the text came out.

"Cut off at 12,000 feet, above the storm. Proceeding due west toward interior; found we had been carried above sea. No visibility below. Impossible know if still flying over sea. Report if storm extends interior."

By reason of the storms the telegram had to be relayed from post to post to Buenos Aires, bearing its message through the night like balefires lit from tower to tower.

Buenos Aires transmitted a reply. "Storm covers all interior area. How much gasoline left?"

"For thirty minutes." These words sped back from post to post to Buenos Aires.

In under half an hour the plane was doomed to plunge into a cyclone which would crash it to the earth.

XVIII

Rivière was musing, all hope lost; somewhere this plane would founder in the darkness. A picture rose in his mind of a scene which had impressed him in his boyhood; a pond that was being emptied to find a body. Thus, till this flood of darkness had been drained off the earth and daylight turned toward the plains and cornfields, nothing would be found. Then some humble peasants perhaps would come on two young bodies, their elbows folded on their faces, like children asleep amid the grass and gold of some calm scene. Drowned by the night.

Rivière thought of all the treasure buried in the depths of night, as in deep, legendary seas. Night's apple trees that wait upon the dawn with all their flowers that serve as yet no purpose. Night, perfume-laden, that hides the lambs asleep and flowers that have no color yet.

Little by little the lush tilth, wet woods, and dew-cool meadows would swing toward the light. But somewhere in the hills, no longer dark with menace, amid the fields and flocks, a world at peace again, two children would seem to sleep. And something would have flowed out of the seen world into that other.

Rivière knew all the tenderness of Fabien's wife, the fears that haunted her; this love seemed only lent her for a while, like a toy to some poor child. He thought of Fabien's hand which, firm on the controls, would hold the balance of his fate some minutes yet; that hand had given caresses and lingered on a breast, wakening a tumult there; a hand of godlike virtue, it had touched a face, transfiguring it. A hand that brought miracles to pass.

Fabien was drifting now in the vast splendor of a sea of clouds, but under him there lay eternity. Among the constellations still he had his being, their only denizen. For yet a while he held the universe in his hand, weighed it at his breast. That wheel he clutched upbore a load of human treasure and desperately, from one star to the other, he trafficked this useless wealth, soon to be his no more.

A single radio post still heard him. The only link between him and the world was a wave of music, a minor modulation. Not a lament, no cry, yet purest of sounds that ever spoke despair.

XIX

Robineau broke in upon his thoughts.

"I've been thinking, sir. . . . Perhaps we might try—"

He had nothing really to suggest but thus proclaimed his good intentions. A solution, how he would have rejoiced to find it! He went about it as if it were a puzzle to be solved. Solutions were his *forte*, but Rivière would not hear of them. "I tell you, Robineau, in life there are no solutions. There are only motive forces, and our task is to set them acting—then the solutions follow." The only force that Robineau had to activate was one which functioned in the mechanics' shop; a humble force which saved propeller-bosses from rusting.

But this night's happenings found Robineau at fault. His inspectorial mandate could not control the elements, nor yet a phantom ship that, as things were, struggled no longer to win a punctuality bonus but only to evade a penalty which canceled all that Robineau imposed, the penalty of death.

There was no use for Robineau now and he roamed the offices, forlorn.

Rivière was informed that Fabien's wife wished to see him. Tormented by anxiety, she was waiting in the clerks' office till Rivière could receive her. The employees were stealing glances at her face. She felt shy, almost shamefast, and gazed nervously around her; she had no right of pres-

ence here. They went about their tasks as usual
and to her it was as if they were trampling on
a corpse; in their ledgers no human sorrow but
dwindled to dross of brittle figures. She looked
for something that might speak to her of Fabien;
at home all things confessed his absence—the
sheets turned back upon the bed, the coffee on
the table, a vase of flowers. Here there was nothing of him; all was at war with pity, friendship,
memories. The only word she caught (for in her
presence they instinctively lowered their voices)
was the oath of an employee clamoring for an
invoice. "The dynamo account, God blast you!
The one we send to Santos." Raising her eyes she
gazed toward this man with a look of infinite
wonder. Then to the wall where a map hung.
Her lips trembled a little, almost imperceptibly.

The realization irked her that in this room she
was the envoy of a hostile creed and almost she
regretted having come; she would have liked to
hide somewhere and, fearful of being remarked,
dared neither cough nor weep. She felt her
presence here misplaced, indecent, as though she
were standing naked before them. But so potent
was *her* truth, the truth within her, that furtively
their eyes strayed ever and again in her direction,
trying to read it on her face. Beauty was hers
and she stood for a holy thing, the world of
human happiness. She vouched for the sanctity
of that material something with which man tam-
pers when he acts. She closed her eyes before
their crowded scrutiny, revealing all the peace
which in his blindness man is apt to shatter.

Rivière admitted her.

So now she was come to make a timid plea for her flowers, the coffee waiting on the table, her own young body. Again, in this room, colder even than the others, her lips began to quiver. Thus, too, she bore witness to her truth, unutterable in this alien world. All the wild yearning of her love, her heart's devotion, seemed here invested with a selfish, pestering aspect. And again she would have liked to leave this place.

"I am disturbing you—"

"No," said Rivière, "you are not disturbing me. But unfortunately neither you nor I can do anything except—wait."

There was a faint movement of her shoulders and Rivière guessed its meaning. "What is the use of that lamp, the dinner waiting, and the flowers there when I return?" Once a young mother had confided in Rivière. "I've hardly realized my baby's death as yet. It's the little things that are so cruel—when I see the baby clothes I had ready, when I wake up at night and there rises in my heart a tide of love, useless now, like my milk . . . all useless!" And for this woman here, Fabien's death would only just begin tomorrow—in every action, useless now, in trivial objects . . . useless. Little by little Fabien would leave his home. A deep, unuttered pity stirred in Rivière's heart.

"Madame—"

The young wife turned and left him with a weak smile, an almost humble smile, ignoring her own power.

Rivière sat down again rather heavily. "Still she is helping me to discover the thing I'm looking for."

He fingered absent-mindedly the messages from the northern airports. "We do not pray for immortality," he thought, "but only not to see our acts and all things stripped suddenly of all their meaning; for then it is the utter emptiness of everything reveals itself."

His gaze fell on the telegrams.

"These are the paths death takes to enter here —messages that have lost their meaning."

He looked at Robineau. Meaningless, too, this fellow who served no purpose now. Rivière addressed him almost gruffly.

"Have I got to tell you what your duties are?"

Then he pushed open the door that led into the Business Office and saw how Fabien's disappearance was recorded there in signs his wife could not have noticed. The slip marked *R.B.903*, Fabien's machine, was already inserted in the wall index of Unavailable Plant. The clerks preparing the papers for the Europe mail were working slackly, knowing it would be delayed. The airport was ringing up for orders respecting the staff on night duty whose presence was no longer necessary. The functions of life were slowing down. That is death! thought Rivière. His work was like a sailing ship becalmed upon the sea.

He heard Robineau speaking. "Sir, they had only been married six weeks."

"Get on with your work!"

Rivière, watching the clerks, seemed to see beyond them the workmen, mechanics, pilots, all who had helped him in his task, with the faith of men who build. He thought of those little cities of old time where men had murmured of the "Indies," built a ship and freighted it with hopes. That men might see their hope outspread its wings across the sea. All of them magnified, lifted above themselves and saved—by a ship! He thought: The goal, perhaps, means nothing, it is the thing done that delivers man from death. By their ship those men will live.

Rivière, too, would be fighting against death when he restored to those telegrams their full meaning, to these men on night duty their unrest and to his pilots their tragic purpose; when life itself would make his work alive again, as winds restore to life a sailing ship upon the sea.

XX

Commodoro Rivadavia could hear nothing now, but twenty seconds later, six hundred miles away, Bahia Blanca picked up a second message.

"Coming down. Entering the clouds. . . . "

Then two words of a blurred message were caught at Trelew.

". . . see nothing . . ."

Short waves are like that; here they can be caught, elsewhere is silence. Then, for no reason, all is changed. This crew, whose position was unknown, made itself heard by living ears, from somewhere out of space and out of time, and at the radio station phantom hands were tracing a word or two on this white paper.

Had the fuel run out already or was the pilot, before catastrophe, playing his last card: to reach the earth again without a crash?

Buenos Aires transmitted an order to Trelew. "Ask him."

The radio station looked like a laboratory with its nickel and its copper, manometers and sheaves of wires. The operators on duty in their white overalls seemed to be bending silently above some simple experiment. Delicately they touched their instruments, exploring the magnetic sky, dowsers in quest of hidden gold.

"No answer?"

"No answer."

Perhaps they yet might seize upon its way a sound that told of life. If the plane and its lights were soaring up to join the stars, it might be they would hear a sound—a singing star!

The seconds flowed away, like ebbing blood. Were they still in flight? Each second killed a hope. The stream of time was wearing life away. As for twenty centuries it beats against a temple, seeping through the granite, and spreads the fane in ruin, so centuries of wear and tear were thronging in each second, menacing the airmen.

Every second swept something away; Fabien's voice, his laugh, his smile. Silence was gaining ground. Heavier and heavier silence drowned their voices, like a heavy sea.

"One forty," some one murmured. "They're out of fuel. They can't be flying any more."

Then silence.

A dry and bitter taste rose on their lips, like

the dry savor of a journey's end. Something mysterious, a sickening thing, had come to pass. And all the shining nickel and trellised copper seemed tarnished with the gloom that broods on ruined factories. All this apparatus had grown clumsy, futile, out of use; a tangle of dead twigs.

One thing remained; to wait for daybreak. In a few hours all Argentina would swing toward the sun, and here these men were standing, as on a beach, facing the net that was being slowly, slowly drawn in toward them, none knowing what its take would be.

To Rivière in his office came that quiet aftermath which follows only on great disasters, when destiny has spent its force. He had set the police of the entire country on the alert. He could do no more; only wait.

But even in the house of death order must have its due. Rivière signed to Robineau.

"Circular telegram to the northern airports. *Considerable delay anticipated Patagonia mail. To avoid undue delay Europe mail, will ship Patagonia traffic on following Europe mail.*"

He stooped a little forward. Then, with an effort, he called something to mind, something important. Yes, that was it. Better make sure.

"Robineau!"

"Sir."

"Issue an order, please. Pilots forbidden to exceed 1900 revs. They're ruining my engines."

"Very good, sir."

Rivière bowed his head a little more. To be alone—that was his supreme desire.

"That's all, Robineau. Trot off, old chap!"

And this, their strange equality before the shades, filled Robineau with awe.

XXI

Robineau was drifting aimlessly about the office. He felt despondent. The company's life had come to a standstill, since the Europe mail, due to start at two, would be countermanded and only leave at daybreak. Morosely the employees kept their posts, but their presence now was purposeless. In steady rhythm the weather reports from the north poured in, but their "no wind," "clear sky," "full moon," evoked the vision of a barren kingdom. A wilderness of stones and moonlight. As Robineau, hardly aware what he was up to, was turning over the pages of a file on which the office superintendent was at work, he suddenly grew conscious that the official in question was at his side, waiting with an air of mocking deference to get his papers back. As if he were saying: "That's my show. Suppose you leave me to it, eh?"

Shocked though he was by his subordinate's demeanor, the inspector found himself tongue-tied and, with a movement of annoyance, handed back the documents. The superintendent resumed his seat with an air of grand punctilio. "I should have told him to go to the devil," thought Robineau. Then, to save his face, he moved away and his thoughts returned to the night's tragedy. For with this tragedy all his chief's campaign went under and Robineau lamented a twofold loss.

The picture of Rivière alone there in his private office rose in Robineau's mind; "old chap," Rivière had said. Never had there been a man so utterly unfriended as he, and Robineau felt an infinite compassion for him. He turned over in his mind vague sentences that hinted sympathy and consolation, and the impulse prompting him struck Robineau as eminently laudable. He knocked gently at the door. There was no answer. Not daring in such a silence to knock louder, he turned the handle. Rivière was there. For the first time Robineau entered Rivière's room almost on an equal footing, almost as a friend; he likened himself to the N.C.O. who joins his wounded general under fire, follows him in defeat and, in exile, plays a brother's part. "Whatever happens I am with you"—that was Robineau's unspoken message.

Rivière said nothing; his head was bowed and he was staring at his hands. Robineau's courage ebbed and he dared not speak; the old lion daunted him, even in defeat. Phrases of loyalty, of ever-growing fervor, rose to his lips; but every time he raised his eyes they encountered that bent head, gray hair, and lips tight-set upon their bitter secret. At last he summoned up his courage.

"Sir!"

Rivière raised his head and looked at him. So deep, so far away had been his dream that till now he might well have been unconscious of Robineau's presence there. And what he felt, what was that dream, and what his heart's bereavement, none would ever know. . . . For a long while Rivière looked at Robineau as at the living witness of some dark event. Robineau felt ill at ease. An enigmatic irony seemed to shape itself on his chief's lips as he watched Robineau. And the longer his chief watched him, the more deeply Robineau blushed and the more it grew on Rivière that this fellow had come, for all his touching and unhappily sincere good will, to act as spokesman for the folly of the herd.

Robineau by now had quite lost his bearings. The N.C.O., the general, the bullets—all faded into mist. Something inexplicable was in the air. Rivière's eyes were still intent on him. Reluctantly he shifted his position, withdrew his hand from his pocket. Rivière's eyes were on him still. At last, hardly knowing what he said, he stammered a few words.

"I've come for orders, sir."

Composedly Rivière pulled out his watch. "It is two. The Asuncion mail will land at two ten. See that the Europe mail takes off at two fifteen."

Robineau bruited abroad the astounding news; the night flight would continue. He accosted the office superintendent.

"Bring me that file of yours to check."

The superintendent brought the papers.

"Wait!"

And the superintendent waited.

XXII

The Asuncion mail signaled that it was about to land. Even at the darkest hour, Rivière had followed, telegram by telegram, its well-ordered

progress. In the turmoil of this night he hailed it
as the avenger of his faith, an all-conclusive witness. Each message telling of this auspicious
flight augured a thousand more such flights to
come. "And, after all," thought Rivière, "we don't
get a cyclone every night! Once the trail is blazed,
it must be followed up."

Coming down, flight by flight, from Paraguay,
as from an enchanted garden set with flowers,
low houses, and slow waters, the pilot had just
skirted the edge of a cyclone which never masked
from him a single star. Nine passengers, huddled
in their traveling-rugs, had pressed their fore-
heads on the window, as if it were a shop front
glittering with gems. For now the little towns of
Argentina were stringing through the night their
golden beads, beneath the paler gold of the star
cities. And at his prow the pilot held within his
hands his freight of lives, eyes wide open, full of
moonlight, like a shepherd. Already Buenos Aires
was dyeing the horizon with pink fires, soon to
flaunt its diadem of jewels, like some fairy hoard.
The wireless operator strummed with nimble
fingers the final telegrams, last notes of a sonata
he had played *allegro* in the sky—a melody
familiar to Rivière's ears. Then he pulled up the
aerial and stretched his limbs, yawning and smiling; another journey done.

The pilot who had just made land greeted the
pilot of the Europe mail, who was lolling, his
hands in his pockets, against the plane.

"Your turn to carry on?"

"Yes."

"Has the Patagonia come in?"

"We don't expect it; lost. How's the weather? Fine?"

"Very fine. Is Fabien lost then?"

They spoke few words of him, for that deep fraternity of theirs dispensed with phrases.

The transit mailbags from Asuncion were loaded into the Europe mail while the pilot, his head bent back and shoulders pressed against the cockpit, stood motionless, watching the stars. He felt a vast power stirring in him and a potent joy.

"Loaded?" some one asked. "Then, contact!"

The pilot did not move. His engine was started. Now he would feel in his shoulders that pressed upon it the airplane come to life. At last, after all those false alarms—to start or not to start—his mind was easy. His lips were parted and in the moon his keen white teeth glittered like a jungle cub's.

"Watch out! The night, you know . . . !"

He did not hear his comrade's warning. His hands thrust in his pockets and head bent back, he stared toward the clouds, mountains and seas and rivers, and laughed silently. Soft laughter that rustled through him like a breeze across a tree, and all his body thrilled with it. Soft laughter, yet stronger, stronger far, than all those clouds and mountains, seas and rivers.

"What's the joke?"

"It's that damned fool Rivière, who said . . . who thinks I've got the wind up!"

XXIII

In a minute he would be leaving Buenos Aires and Rivière, on active service once again, wanted to hear him go. To hear his thunder rise and swell and die into the distance like the tramp of armies marching in the stars.

With folded arms Rivière passed among the clerks and halted at a window to muse and listen. If he had held up even one departure, that would be an end of night flights. But, by launching this other mail into the darkness, Rivière had forestalled the weaklings who tomorrow would disclaim him.

Victory, defeat—the words were meaningless. Life lies behind these symbols and life is ever bringing new symbols into being. One nation is weakened by a victory, another finds new forces in defeat. Tonight's defeat conveyed perhaps a lesson which would speed the coming of final victory. The work in progress was all that mattered.

Within five minutes the radio stations would broadcast the news along the line, and across a thousand miles the vibrant force of life would give pause to every problem.

Already a deep organ note was booming; the plane.

Rivière went back to his work and, as he passed, the clerks quailed under his stern eyes; Rivière the Great, Rivière the Conqueror, bearing his heavy load of victory.